Pardon Me...
Is That The Chattanooga Choo-Choo?

by Ellen Eady

illustrated by Kelly Guhne

Majestic Publishing • Chattanooga

In memory of Barbara Allen Eady - E.E.

With love to my nieces and nephew, Lauren, Megan, Sarah and Steve. - K.G.

Text edited by Jim Stover
Story edited by Ann Upton
Library of Congress Control Number: 00-090493
ISBN: 0-9679065-0-4 (Hard cover)
ISBN: 0-9679065-1-2 (Paperback)
Majestic Publishing
1303 Hixson Pike, Suite A
Chattanooga, TN 37405
Printed in the United States of America
Second printing

Harry the hopping mouse was packing for summer vacation. He was traveling halfway around the world from his home in Australia to Chattanooga, Tennessee. The family would be staying at the historic Chattanooga Choo-Choo. It was a railroad station about 100 years ago, but now it's a famous hotel. They would even be staying in a real sleeping car!

When they arrived at the Chattanooga airport, Harry and his family rushed to the baggage claim area. There was a lot of noise and confusion. Harry began playing on the luggage carousel, even when his mother told him not to.

He was still playing when his mother called for him to get into the taxicab. Harry grabbed his backpack and jumped into the yellow taxi. The wrong yellow taxi!

Realizing his mistake, Harry scrambled to look out the window. He watched helplessly as the taxi pulled away from the curb. Horrified, Harry wondered where the taxi would take him.

After 30 minutes, the yellow taxi came to a screeching halt. Harry tumbled out of the cab and was greeted by a gnome standing on a rock. Behind him was a quaint stone building.

"Pardon me, gnome," Harry said. "Is that the Chattanooga Choo-Choo?"
"Oh no," giggled the gnome. "That's Rock City. You should see it."

Harry took the gnome's advice and wandered through the maze
of rocks. He teetered across the Swing-Along-Bridge...

and inched through
Fat Man's Squeeze.

At the gift shop, Harry saw a little boy buying a birdhouse. Suddenly, he had an idea. Maybe this boy was going to the Chattanooga Choo-Choo! He sneaked inside the birdhouse and waited.

Harry jiggled and joggled inside the birdhouse. He peeked outside, just as the boy stepped onto an elevator. As the elevator slowly descended, Harry's ears began to pop like corn. At last the doors slid open. Harry peered out for another look when he heard a thunderous roar.

He almost fell off the birdhouse when he saw a towering waterfall cascading deep inside a cavern. Spray misted his fur as he gawked at the incredible sight. Fearful of being discovered, Harry ducked back into his hideout.

He was startled when a nosy bird poked her beak inside. "Good heavens," she chirped. "A little bird told me this birdhouse was available." She pushed her way in and fluffed her feathers.

"Pardon me, ma'am," Harry said politely.

"I can't fly another foot with my bad wing," she continued.

"Pardon me, ma'am," Harry persisted, "but is that the Chattanooga Choo-Choo?"

"Goodness, no," she cackled. "That's Ruby Falls. You're 1100 feet underground, Sonny! But you'd better stay inside if you don't want to look like a wet rat."

"I'll keep that in mind," Harry promised.

"Remember, I have first dibs on this place!" With that, the bird turned and wiggled back through the opening. Her plump bottom wedged in the hole, and she squawked noisily. "Help! I'm stuck!"

Harry backed up and plowed into the bird's rump.

"Have a nice flight," he cheered.

The next time Harry crawled out of the
birdhouse, he saw a fortress with iron gates
and cannons. He walked through the gates
and found a soldier on duty.

"Pardon me, corporal," inquired Harry, "is
that the Chattanooga Choo-Choo?"
"No, SIR!" shouted the corporal. "This is
Point Park, SIR! Lookout point for the
Confederate Army, SIR!"
"Well, ah, where would I find the Chattanooga
Choo-Choo, corporal?"
"In the valley, SIR!"
Harry looked out over the edge of the
mountain and scratched his head.
"How do I get down the mountain, corporal?"
"Take The Incline, SIR!" the soldier announced.

Harry followed the corporal's directions and found The Incline. It was a railway car that took passengers up and down Lookout Mountain. The conductor told Harry that it was the steepest passenger incline in the world. That didn't surprise Harry. He curled his tail around a railing so he wouldn't fall off the seat.

When Harry stepped off The Incline, he spotted another taxicab at the curb. He hopped in and felt his stomach churn with excitement. Maybe it would take him to his family. Minutes later the taxi stopped in front of an amazing building. Fountains, streams and trees surrounded it. Harry was hot, so he jumped out of the taxi and into the fountains. After cooling off, he approached a tourist taking pictures of the building.

"Pardon me, Ma'am," he interrupted. "Is that the Chattanooga Choo-Choo?"
"No, my dear," the woman replied with a smile. "That's the Tennessee Aquarium. It's a huge tank for freshwater wildlife. I have an extra ticket that you can use."
"Oh, thank you, Ma'am!" Harry said.

Harry entered the giant aquarium and explored the freshwater habitat. He was waving to a scuba diver swimming with the fish when a giant catfish appeared from out of nowhere and swam right toward him. It weighed almost 70 pounds! Harry left the building immediately. He was afraid of cats!

After his scare, Harry wandered through downtown Chattanooga. He stumbled upon the Creative Discovery Museum and was swept inside with a whole kindergarten class as they marched through the doors with their teacher.

Harry visited every room in the museum. He was amazed at all the experiments he could conduct. But his favorite activity was digging up bones in the dinosaur pit. What fun! They even gave him tools to excavate the fossils.

Even though Harry was a hopping mouse, his legs felt tired. He noticed an Imax 3-D Theater on the corner and decided to go inside for a rest. His 3-D glasses were too big, but he managed to make them fit. As he nibbled his popcorn, he marveled at how real the movie seemed. Once Harry even thought the shark onscreen was going to eat him. As the shark swam closer, Harry panicked and flipped out of his chair. Embarrassed, he grabbed his backpack and fled the theater.

Harry hopped around anxiously until he caught a glimpse of a beautiful blue bridge! It was the Walnut Street Bridge, the longest pedestrian bridge in the world. He decided to cross it to the other side.

Bad idea for a little mouse! He ended up dodging strollers, roller blades, bicycles, joggers, and more!

On the way over, Harry noticed a shimmering golden horse atop a building down below. He decided to investigate. He discovered a pavilion with beautifully carved animals that moved up and down and round and round. A lady was collecting tokens to ride the animals. Harry tugged on the lady's skirt until she looked down at him. "Pardon me, lady...is that the Chattanooga Choo-Choo?"

"Not quite," she laughed. "This is the Coolidge Park Carousel. If you buy a token, you can ride your favorite animal."

Harry reached into his backpack and dug out some change. He found an ostrich to ride and climbed onto his back. As the music played, Harry rode the giant bird around and around and around.

After several minutes Harry felt very dizzy. He hopped off the bird and wobbled to the riverbank to get some fresh air. As he started feeling better, he heard a strange sound.

"Psst. Psst."
It was echoing from underneath the bridge. Harry looked up and spied a rock climber pulling himself up a column on the bridge. The climber's name was Mike. He dared Harry to climb the famous Walnut Wall.

Harry put on climbing gear and raced his challenger up the stony mass. His legs were stronger than Mike's, and he won with ease.

Mike handed a piece of cheese to Harry. "Here, dude. You could use some fuel after that awesome climb."

Harry was starving. He popped the cheese into his mouth and swallowed it whole. Then he looked out over the Tennessee River and noticed for the first time a cluster of old mansions perched on a bluff.

"Pardon me, dude," Harry said to Mike. "Is that the Chattanooga Choo-Choo?"

"No way, mouse-dude. That's the art district. You should check it out. There are museums, restaurants, a sculpture garden, and my personal favorite...the pastry chef's window."

"How do I get there?" Harry asked.

"It's easy-peasy, man. Just cross back over the Walnut Street Bridge and follow the Riverwalk. It winds underneath the bridge and up the bluff."

"Thank you," Harry said graciously.

"You are very welcome, little mouse-dude."

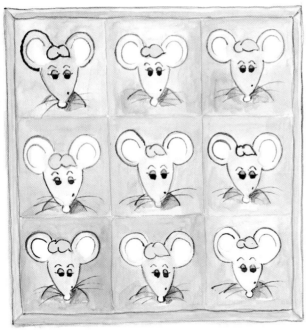

Harry enjoyed the twists and turns leading to the art district. He admired the art at the Hunter Museum and the unusual sculptures at the Sculpture Garden.

Harry was even inspired to create his own sculpture. He called it "Stinky Cheese."

Stinky Cheeze

Harry finally passed the window where the pastry chef was creating delicious works of bakery art. He sampled a little bit of...everything!

With his tummy full and his legs tired, Harry began to feel sleepy. He noticed an empty coffee can on the side of the street and crawled inside for a rest.

It was peaceful inside until a street sweeper swept him up and slung him down the hill. The can rolled faster and faster until, CRASH, it hit a curb. Harry was launched out of the can and into the road.

He screamed when he saw an electric bus heading right for him. Harry rolled quickly out of the way and just missed being a mouse-track.

By now, Harry was very anxious to find his
family. He boarded the same Carta Shuttle bus
that had nearly mowed him down and toured
the city. It was free!

Harry sat quietly on the bus and thought about his predicament.
He missed his parents and his sister Hattie. If only he hadn't
misbehaved on the luggage carousel. If only he hadn't gotten into
the wrong taxi. If only...Harry closed his eyes and started to sniffle.

Just then, the bus driver made an announcement. In a deep, southern drawl he said the sweetest words Harry had ever heard. "Next stop, the Chattanooga Choo-Choo."

Harry's wet eyes popped open. He leaped for the cord next to his seat and swung on it till the bell rang.

When the bus finally stopped, Harry jumped out and burst through the doors of the hotel. He anxiously searched the historic lobby. He found his family at the concierge's desk. His mother was sobbing, her face in her paws. His father stood sadly next to her, holding Hattie.

"Mom! Dad! Hattie!" Harry yelled. He jumped into his mother's arms.
"Harry found us!" Hattie cried.
His mother squeezed him tight as she stroked his fur. "Oh, Harry," she whispered, "we were so worried."

"Let's get a good night's sleep, son," his dad said, patting his head.
"Tomorrow we'll show you the sights."